Shopping for Snowflakes

BY MARCIA LEONARD
PICTURES BY JOHN HIMMELMAN

Silver Press

For Precious Rusty Berkower.
— M.L.

To my brother Joe, one of my two closest friends in the world.
— J.H.

Library of Congress Cataloging-in-Publication Data

Leonard, Marcia.
     Shopping for snowflakes / by Marcia Leonard;
pictures by John Himmelman.
          p.   cm. — (What next?)
     Summary: Since they are out of bread, Rabbit and
Hare go to the grocery store and indulge in a shopping
spree. At various points in the text the reader is asked to
guess what happens next.
     [1. Rabbits—Fiction.   2. Hares—Fiction.
3. Shopping—Fiction.   4. Literary recreations.]
I. Himmelman, John, ill.   II. Title.   III. Series:
Leonard, Marcia. What next?
PZ7.L549Sh   1989
[E]—dc19   89-6009
                                                        CIP
ISBN 0-671-68594-5 ISBN 0-671-68590-2 (lib. bdg.)   AC

Produced by Small Packages, Inc.
Text copyright © 1989 Small Packages, Inc.

Illustrations copyright © 1989 Small Packages, Inc.
and John Himmelman.

Published by Silver Press, a division of
Silver Burdett Press, Inc.
Simon & Schuster, Inc.
Prentice Hall Bldg., Englewood Cliffs, NJ 07632.

Printed in the United States of America.

10   9   8   7   6   5   4   3   2   1

Rabbit and Hare were making sandwiches for lunch.
"We have plenty of cheese," said Rabbit,
"but I can't find the bread. Do you know where it is?"

"Yes," said Hare. "It's in my tummy.
I ate the last two slices for breakfast."
"Oh, dear," said Rabbit.
"We can't make sandwiches without bread."

So what do you think Rabbit and Hare did next?

Did they go to a toy store and buy some balloons?

Did they visit the North Pole to shop for snowflakes?

Did they drive to the grocery store to get some bread?

Or did they sail to the seashore to pick up sand?

Rabbit and Hare hopped into their car and drove to the grocery store. "You can stay here," said Rabbit. "I'll just run in and buy the bread."

"Wait," said Hare. "I'm coming, too. I might
see something else I'd like for lunch."

The store was having a special sale on cookies. Soon Rabbit and Hare had their arms full. "We need something to carry these packages," said Rabbit.

Now what do you think they decided to use —

a shiny metal grocery cart,

a bright orange dump truck,

a delicate silver teaspoon,

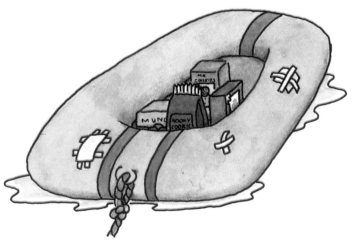

or a leaky rubber raft?

Rabbit and Hare put their cookies into the grocery cart and pushed it down the aisle.
"Look at the beautiful lettuce," said Hare.
"We could make a salad to go with our sandwiches!"

"Good idea," said Rabbit. "Let's have tomatoes, too."
"And carrots and cucumbers and celery," said Hare.

They put the vegetables into their cart and went
to look at the apples. "Would you like red ones
or green ones?" asked Rabbit.
"Both," said Hare, and he picked up two of each kind.

Then what do you think Hare did with the apples?

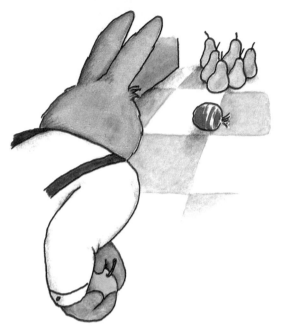

Did he roll them down the aisle of the store?

Did he put them into the shopping cart?

Did he juggle them high in the air?

Or did he draw a little face on each one?

Hare put the apples into the cart, and he
and Rabbit went all through the store.
They stopped at the dairy case to get a carton of milk.

Then they took their cart to the check-out counter.

Rabbit paid for the groceries, and Hare helped the clerk put everything into three big brown bags.

Now what do you think Rabbit and Hare did next?

Did they climb into the cart
and wait for a ride?

Did they put all of the food
back on the shelves?

Did they have a picnic on
the grocery store floor?

Or did they put the bags in
their car and drive home?

Rabbit and Hare drove home and unpacked their groceries. They made a salad, poured themselves some milk, and set aside the apples and cookies for dessert.

"Lunch at last," said Hare, "and everything looks so tasty!"
"Yes," said Rabbit. "There's only one problem . . . ."

"We forgot to buy the bread!"